# WHO'S TO SAY...?

WRITTEN BY
**DEVEN TELLIS, Ed.D**

ILLUSTRATED BY
COURTNEY MONDAY

# Dedication

*To Adrien & Rhyann,*
*With all my love…*

*Here's hoping that you are as proud*
*of me as I am of you both.*

*Let this book be proof that our dreams*
*can come true if only we have the faith*
*and courage to pursue them.*

# Acknowledgments

*A million thank yous to my sister,*
*Deidra, for being my encourager,*
*sounding board, and biggest fan*
*throughout this process. I could not*
*have done this without you!*

Who's to say...
That I can't sing?

Well, I can!
I will sing my song
anyway.

Who's to say...
That I can't dance?

Because I can!
I will always move to
the beat of my own
music.

Who's to say...
That I can't speak?

Yes, I can!
I will continue to use
my voice to speak up
and speak out.

Who's to say...
That I can't write?

Well, I can!
I'm going to be the great author of my very own story.

Who's to say...
That I can't travel the world?

Oh, but I can!
I will forever embrace learning about new people and new cultures.

Who's to say...
That I can't be a boss?

Sure, I can!
I will continue to lead by
example and serve
others.

Who's to say...
That I can't be a
game-changer?

Of course, I can!
I will work hard and think
outside the box.

Who's to say...
That I am not athletic?

Oh, yes, I am!
I will skillfully exercise my
mind and body to prepare for
any competition.

# Who's to say...
# That I'm not a winner?

Well, I am!
I will always continue to rise to the top and reach my highest goals.

Who's to say...
That I'm not smart?

In fact, I am!
I will learn all I can while
working towards my
bright future.

Who's to say…
That I am not a
friend?

Yes, I am!
I will always be kind
and uphold the
Golden Rule.

# Who's to say...
# That I'm not beautiful?

**Indeed, I am!
I will forever be
proud of who I
was created to be.**

**Now, who *really* is to say...**
**What I can or cannot be?**
**Who I can or cannot be?**

**Why not a singing, dancing motivational speaker, a prize-winning writer, or a world-class athlete? Why not a game-changing boss who is equally smart and friendly...Or simply a beautiful soul with goals and dreams?**

Why, NO ONE, of course!!!
Not. A. Single. Person.
At the end of the day,
absolutely no one is to
say...

No one...except ME!!!
Only I can say what I can
and cannot do.
Only I can say what I am
or what I am not.

I am my BIGGEST fan.
I BELIEVE in ME.

Made in the USA
Columbia, SC
16 July 2021